THE ADVENTURES OF PELICAN PETE

ANNIE THE RIVER OTTER

FRANCES KEISER

ILLUSTRATED BY HUGH KEISER

Sagaponack Books • Saint Augustine

We wish to acknowledge the following experts for their accuracy checks:

Jan Reed-Smith, North American River Otter Liaison, The World Conservation Union, Species Survival Commission (IUCN/SSC) Otter Specialist Group; American Zoo and Aquarium Association (AZA) Otter Species Survival Plan (SSP) N. A. River Otter Advisor

Melanie Cain-Stage, North American River Otter Rehabilitation Specialist; President, Humane Association of Wildlife Care and Education (H.A.W.K.E.) HawkeWildlife.org

John Owens, Fire Education Specialist, National Interagency Fire Center, Bureau of Land Management

Mark Kaib, Fire Ecologist, U.S. Fish and Wildlife Service

Elaine Thrune, Wildlife Rehabilitator, Founding Board Member and Past President of the National Wildlife Rehabilitators Association

Jodi Beck Witte, Veterinary Medical Assistance Team Member (VMAT), Large Animal Rescuer, Wildlife Rehabilitator, animalhelp.com

Thanks to:

Family, friends, and colleagues who freely gave their support, advice, and expertise; children, parents, grandparents, and teachers who enthusiastically provided opinions and encouragement; experts on the areas of otters, wildland fires, and wildlife rehabilitation who so generously gave their time and knowledge; and especially to Jae Bass, Jim Collis, Tara Dunn, Beth Mansbridge, and Veronica Moore.

Keiser, Frances.
    Annie the river otter / by Frances Keiser; Illustrated by Hugh Keiser — 1st. ed.
    1 v. (unpaged) : col. ill., ; 26 cm.
    (The adventures of Pelican Pete ; 4)
       SUMMARY: Pelican Pete befriends a young river otter and takes her to a rehabilitator after she is hurt escaping a wildland fire.
    Audience: Ages 4-8.
    ISBN 978-0-9668845-4-8
    [1. Otters—Fiction. 2. Pelicans—Fiction. 3. Wildfires—Fiction. 4. Wildlife rehabilitation—Fiction 4. Stories in rhyme] I. Keiser, Hugh, ill. II. Title: Annie the river otter

PZ8.3.K273An 2006
[E]—dc22   2005934335
2006

For the wildlife rehabilitators: the dedicated women and men who work tirelessly to rescue, nurse, and rehabilitate injured, sick, and orphaned wildlife.

"Start by doing what's necessary; then do what's possible; and suddenly you are doing the impossible."
—St. Francis of Assisi

Also in the Pelican Pete Series:

A Bird Is Born
Preening For Flight
First Discoveries
Un Ave Nace (Spanish)

Member of the Green Press Initiative
Printed on Recycled Paper

For all the children good and sweet:
I'll tell a tale of Pelican Pete;
And for all who were *bad* today:
I'll tell the story anyway.

Pete's a bird who's fun to know,
Having adventures high and low.
So let's join Pete and follow his trail
From an island, where we start our tale. . . .

Preening and resting on the river shore,
With ocean waves a distant roar,
Pete's watching the current drift slowly by
When suddenly a movement catches his eye.

What is that? Something curious
Is swimming toward him fast and furious;
Coming near, now he can spot her.
Poor little thing: it's a young river otter.

The small, brown creature climbs onto dry land
So tired and wobbly she can hardly stand.
Pete goes to her, full of concern.
Is she all right? He has to learn!

"Where's your mother? Are you alone?
Are you hurt? Have you broken a bone?
Are you bleeding? Are you being chased?
What happened to you? What have you faced?"

She looks up at Pete, feeling scared and weak,
And knows his meaning though he didn't speak.
Animals can't talk the way you and I do;
They communicate differently, and understand too.

"My name is Annie. I barely escaped.
My paw is cut; my skin is scraped.
My family is missing; I can't go back home.
I've no place to go and now I'm alone."

"Don't worry, Annie, I'll be your friend.
Your cut will heal; your scrape will mend.
My name's Pete. Here, sit under this tree.
Rest for awhile; tell your story to me."

Annie's story:

My parents met on the river shore
And built a den for three or four
Hidden in the roots of a riverbank tree
With a bed of soft grasses for Brother and me.

Born as the weather is just turning warm,
Mom feeds us and cleans us and keeps us from harm.
At two months old I can walk and climb,
And we leave the den for the very first time.

This is our territory to scout and roam;
Each day we go a little farther from home.
"Stay close to me," Mom barks in warning
As we venture out one early morning.

Everything is new: so strange and alluring.
I'm having an adventure: I love exploring!
Bouncing and hopping, I'm an excited pup.
I chirp, "Wait for me!" and run to catch up.

Mom calls us to follow and makes a turn;
We have many lessons and skills to learn.
As the cool morning breeze ripples my fur,
Mom stops and whistles us closer to her.

She stands on hind legs, head high in the air,
Looking and sniffing to see what's there.
I follow her lead and stand up tall,
Using tail for a brace so I won't fall.

My whiskers bristle, my nose does a twitch.
The scents in the air are varied and rich
Of animals nearby and ones who passed through—
Friend and foe, old and new.

Mother concludes there's no present danger;
Nothing to fear, no enemy or stranger.
With our den nearby, we continue to ramble
Among colorful flowers and fragrant bramble

Where butterflies flutter, dragonflies dance,
And birds fly by without a glance.
Hungry ducks tip their tails,
And little frogs leap across the trails.

Then back to the den, where I nap for the day
And dream happy dreams of running and play.
When I awake, my stomach is growling;
I wonder what Mother caught while prowling.

She hunts for food and brings it home;
Now we have to learn to catch our own.
While crunchy crayfish are a tasty treat,
Fresh fish are my *favorite* food to eat.

But they live in the river and I won't go in;
I'm afraid of the water and I can't swim.
Mother will teach us; it's our lesson today.
Entering the water, she leads the way.

Paddling with ease, Mom shows us how.
Then she calls us to follow. It's our turn now.
Brother is brave and runs down the hill,
But he knocks me over and I take a spill.

Slipping and sliding, in the water I'm thrown,
Will I sink to the bottom just like a stone?
Mom comes to my rescue, diving below,
And, holding her fur, to the surface we go.

Reaching the air, I breathe and I wonder
How to kick my legs so I don't go under.
Mother and Brother show how it's done;
Soon I can do it, and it's so much fun!

My webbed paws I use like paddles and fins,
My tail like a rudder for dives and spins.
I learn to dip and dart and race,
And now I'm swimming all over the place.

But the best part of all is making a slide
Of slippery mud so we can ride
To the water below . . . Splash! Then we begin
To race up the hill and do it again.

Tag and chase, hide and seek,
Romp and roll, and boo and peek
Are the games we love, the sports we play. . . .
And then it happens: my awful day.

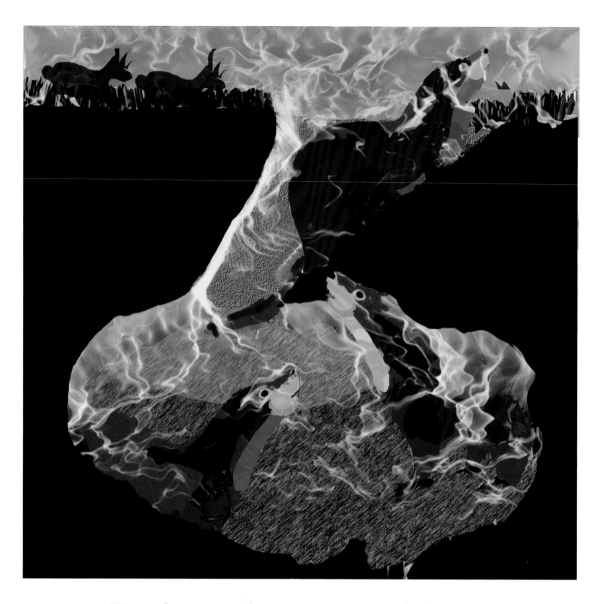

We wake up early to a strange red glare;
The scent of burning wood fills the air.
All the animals are running with fear:
Birds and mice, rabbits and deer.

Mother knows the danger we face;
"Wait here," she cries and turns to race
Outside to find a way to flee.
Brother runs after her. They both leave me!

Something must have happened; they don't return.
The fire is closer and soon it will burn
So near to the den I won't get free.
I must leave *now* and run toward the sea.

The fire is hot. I cough and choke.
Everything is ablaze, and thick black smoke
Stings my eyes so I don't see
A tree crashing down, barely missing me.

I stumble and tumble and fall on my chin,
Cut my paw and scrape my skin,
Roll over a rock, and then, at last,
I land in the water and swim away fast.

"I've come to this island where I found you,
    But now I don't know what to do."
"Don't worry, Annie, I'll help you;
    There's a wonderful place I'll lead you to.

They rescue animals and heal them quick—
Orphaned, stranded, injured, or sick.
When we're in need, we hurry there
For wildlife rescue and animal care.

People work hard to help you get well,
And when you're better, with fond farewell
They set you free in a safe place
Where you can once again play and race.

When your family's found, they'll be there too;
Perhaps they're already waiting for you.
Follow me, Annie, I'll show you the way.
I'm glad we met; you've made my day.

It feels good helping another,
Being a friend, a buddy, a brother.
One of Pete's Pals you'll always be—
A member of my extended family."

The day is ending as Pete takes to wing.
What adventures will tomorrow bring?
Curious birds need to travel and roam,
To fly beyond their familiar home.

Visiting new habitats, towns, and places;
Making new friends, seeing new faces.
There's so much to learn, discover, and see.
With a wing, Pete beckons, "Come along with me!"

Did You Know?

- Otters belong to the same family as ferrets, badgers, minks, and weasels. The scientific name for the North American river otter is *Lontra canadensis*. Order: Carnivora; Family: Mustelidae; Subfamily: Lutrinae; Genus: *Lontra*; Species: *canadensis*.

- The otter's ancestors have been on Earth for 20 million years. Today, there are thirteen species of otters in the world. They are found on every continent except Australia and Antarctica. Two species of otters live in the United States: the sea otter (*Enhydra lutris*) and the North American river otter (*Lontra canadensis*).

- River otters are semiaquatic animals found throughout most of Canada, the United States, and in a few isolated areas of Mexico. They spend about one-third of their time in the water: rivers, lakes, marshes, swamps, or estuaries. River otters are often confused with sea otters, marine mammals that spend all of their time in the sea.

- When full-grown, otters are 35 to 54 inches long and weigh from 10 to 33 pounds. The river otter's tail is 12 to 20 inches long and weighs up to one-third of the animal's total weight.

- Lacking a layer of blubber, otters must rely on their thick fur to keep them warm. The fur is a combination of long, water-repellent guard hairs and short, wool-like underhairs. To trap air and increase insulation, the otters blow air bubbles into their fur, roll on the ground, and groom frequently.

- Otters communicate with many sounds: they whistle, chirp, grunt, growl, chuckle, chatter, snarl, snort, cough, whoop, and scream. They also communicate by touch, body gestures, posture, and leaving a strong musky odor on vegetation.

- Otters' senses of smell and sound are very keen, and their highly sensitive whiskers help them find prey in murky waters by touch. Sight is not a primary sense and they are unable to see clearly in the distance. Little is known about the otter's fifth sense, taste.

- Otters prefer a den abandoned by other animals such as beavers, or they seek a suitable place in tree hollows, rock piles, or logjams. They can have one to six pups, but the usual litter ranges from two to three. At birth, the furry pups, whose eyes and ears are closed, make chirping sounds and weigh about 5 ounces.

- Otters catch their prey, mostly fish and crustaceans, with their mouths. They may also eat insects, frogs, and other reptiles and amphibians, and occasionally small mammals, birds, and fledglings.

- Being active animals, otters digest their food and burn calories quickly. They must eat up to 20 percent of their own body weight each day, which means a 20-pound otter needs to eat about four pounds of fish per day—the equivalent of more than eight Big Macs!

- When they are two or three month old, otters are taught how to swim by there mothers. Mom will throw them into the water and retrieve them, or she will swim with one on her back and dip under water, leaving the pup to paddle on the surface.

- Otters can hold their breath up to four minutes underwater, but most dives last less than one minute. Valves of skin in the nose and ears close to keep water out, and they are able to swim at speeds of up to seven miles per hour.

- Energetic and inquisitive animals, otters love to explore and play. They run, chase, slide, wrestle, and enjoy pushing a twig along the surface of the water with their nose. They are able to pick up small objects like pebbles with their webbed paws to toss, drop in the water, dive for, hide, and find.

- Fun, fast, and effortless, sliding is an efficient way for otters to get around. They love to use slides to get into the water and for traveling on snow. Otters can run with their humpedbacked, loping gait at speeds of up to 18 miles per hour.

- Otters can live to be 15+ years old in the wild and 20+ years in captivity. Humans hunt them for their valuable fur and are responsible for the main dangers to otters: water pollution and habitat destruction.

- In some ways otters and pelicans are alike. They both have webbed feet, eat fish, are very curious, love to play, and have been hunted for their feathers or fur. In some regions they also share the same habitats.

- Fire is an important part of our wildlands, and essential for the survival of many plant and animal species as well as entire ecosystems. Without fire in a natural or prescribed form, species and ecosystems adapted to fire cannot survive. These plants and animals rely on occasional fires to cleanse the ecosystem of dead vegetation, to recycle soil nutrients, and to maintain healthy watersheds.

- Except for nestlings and weak or hurt animals, typically, most animals escape wildfires. They use their adaptations or natural abilities to avoid fires, run away, burrow underground, or hide in caves and other safe places.

- Wild animals that are injured, sick, or orphaned are taken to wildlife rehabilitation facilities. Wildlife rehabilitators are trained and skilled at caring for injured, sick, and orphaned wild animals. When the animals are well and able to survive on their own, they are released back into their natural habitats.

- If you find a sick or injured animal, take note of its location, keep pets away, and call the nearest wildlife rehabilitation facility. The rehabilitator will answer your questions, tell you what to do depending on the animal species and the problem, and help find the best solution.

- Many of the wildlife rehabilitators and the people who work with them are volunteers. They rely on donations from people like you to keep the facilities running and supplied, so support, donate, and volunteer.

- For more fascinating facts about North American river otters, wildland fires and wildfire ecology, and wildlife rehabilitation, visit pelicanpete.com.

To Learn More:

To learn more about otters:

Look for otters near estuaries, streams, lakes, and rivers, especially ones with beavers. Otters may be difficult to spot in the wild, but you can observe them up close at a zoo. You can find a list of zoos exhibiting otters at the American Zoo and Aquarium Association's site: azasweb.com. Go to their cool critters page and click on North American Otter. You may also be able to see otters at a wildlife rehabilitation center (see the information below). Visit your local library or bookstore for books on otters. Some good Web sites with information about otters include: otternet.com, which also hosts the River Otter Alliance, otterjoy.com, or The International Otter Survival Fund at otter.org. For links to these and more sites, visit pelicanpete.com

To learn more about wildland fires:

Visit your local fire department and talk to the firefighters. Universities and county extension offices have information about wildland fires and wildfire ecology. Visit your local library or bookstore for books on wildland fires and wildfire ecology. Search the Internet. Locations for good information about wildland fires include the sites of the National Interagency Fire Center (nifc.gov), National Wildfire Coordinating Group (nwcg.gov), International Association of Wildland Fire (iawfonline.org), Bureau of Land Management Office of Fire and Aviation (fire.blm.gov), USDA Forest Service Fire and Aviation Management (fs.fed.us/fire), The Nature Conservancy Global Fire Network (tncfire.org), the U.S. Fish and Wildlife Service Fire Management (fire.fws.gov), National Park Service Fire Management (nps.gov/fire), and Smokeybear.com. For links to these and more sites, visit pelicanpete.com.

To learn more about wildlife rehabilitators:

A wildlife rehabilitation facility may be close to you no matter where you are in the world. In an emergency, local veterinary hospitals, zoos, aquariums, or law enforcement agencies should be able to tell you where the closest facility is. Visit your local library or bookstore for books on wildlife rehabilitation. If you have access to the Internet, you can learn more and search for rehabilitators at the sites of Animal Help (animalhelp.com), Wildlife International (wildlife-international.org), The Wildlife Rehabilitation Information Directory (tc.umn.edu/~devo0028), National Wildlife Rehabilitators Association (nwrawildlife.org), International Wildlife Rehabilitation Council (iwrc-online.org), the U.S. Fish and Wildlife Service (fws.gov), the International Association of Fish and Wildlife Agencies (iafwa.org), and the wildlife service in your country, state, or province. You'll find links to these and more sites at pelicanpete.com.

Photograph by Oscar Sosa

About the Author and Illustrator:

Hugh Keiser, a graduate of The Cooper Union in New York City, has been painting and drawing for over forty years. He has received many awards and his work is included in numerous public and private collections.

Hugh began to explore the computer as an art medium about the same time he and Frances moved to Florida and fell in love with the brown pelican—the clown prince of birds. Illustrations for a series of books featuring Pelican Pete are the result.

Frances Keiser, naturalist, wildlife rescue volunteer, and friend to animals and children, has worked for the public school system with preschoolers and has conducted children's craft workshops.

Raised on fairy tales, Frances continues to develop her love of children's books by being a collector and avid reader to children. Many of her favorite stories are in rhyme, which influenced her to write her own books in verse.

The Adventures of Pelican Pete books are an accurate and educational depiction of nature, historic and geographic locations, and wildlife. Included in each story is a lesson to aid the safety of our wildlife or environment.

The Keisers live with their two cats, Katie and Sparky, on a barrier island near St. Augustine, Florida, where wildlife abounds, children explore, and curious pelicans fly overhead.

About Sagaponack Books:

Sagaponack Books publishes children's picture books to support Earth's beauty, habitats, and wildlife for continuing generations by helping children understand the natural world and foster a desire to protect it. To learn more, visit SagaponackBooks.com